SCARY SEA STORIES

By Jonathan Schmidt

Interior illustrations
by Warren Chang

A Roxbury Park Book

LOWELL HOUSE JUVENILE

LOS ANGELES

NTC/Contemporary Publishing Group

Cover illustration by Robert Sullivan

Published by Lowell House
A division of NTC/Contemporary Publishing Group, Inc.
4255 West Touhy Avenue, Lincolnwood (Chicago), Illinois 60646-1975 U.S.A.

Lowell House books can be purchased at special discounts when ordered in bulk for premiums and special sales. Contact Department CS at the following address:
NTC/Contemporary Publishing Group
4255 West Touhy Avenue
Lincolnwood, IL 60646-1975
1-800-323-4900

ISBN: 0-7373-0034-5
Library of Congress Catalog Card Number: 98-066684

Roxbury Park is a division of NTC/Contemporary Publishing Group, Inc.

Managing Director and Publisher: Jack Artenstein
Editor in Chief, Roxbury Park Books: Michael Artenstein
Director of Publishing Services: Rena Copperman
Managing Editor: Nicole Monastirsky

Printed and bound in the United States of America
10 9 8 7 6 5 4 3 2

CONTENTS

MILLER'S POINT

BECKA SAT UP in bed. She swung her legs over the side and stretched. It was the first day of summer vacation, and Becka couldn't wait to shower and eat and head down to the beach to meet her friends. This would be the best summer ever. First off, next term she would be a tenth grader. No more baby stuff for her.

Second, it was pretty much common knowledge that Matt Hastings had a crush on her. And Matt was just about the best-looking boy in San Diego.

But best of all, she was part of The Group. Only the prettiest and most popular girls at James Madison were asked to join The Group. The crème de la crème. The elite.

But when she looked over at the guest bed across the room she frowned, as if suddenly remembering something horrible.

Marianne.

Her cousin had arrived last night. She was from Iowa. Becka had never met anyone from Iowa before. Iowa sounded as far away and as bleak as Mars.

A few weeks earlier her mother had asked Becka if it would be all right for Becka's cousin to come and stay the summer. It wasn't fair, Becka whined "You won't have to baby-sit," her mother said. "Marianne is the same age as you. You and she will have a lot in common."

Becka let her chin drop. She rolled her gorgeous blue eyes to the sky and groaned: "Oh really, mother. I mean, have you gone, like, completely eight-track? The little tumor is from Idaho."

"Iowa."

"What . . . *ever.*"

"I want you to be nice to her. Show her around. You two will have loads of fun together. Introduce her to your friends."

"Are you like totally *insane?*" Becka shrieked. "I'd rather die first." This was just the kind of hideous infraction that could get a member expelled from The Group.

"Oh, Becka, quit being so dramatic. Now go upstairs and clean your room. And clear out your closet to make space for Marianne."

"*She's staying in my room?*"

"Yes, dear." The guest room was being refurnished, and Mrs. Hoover didn't want Marianne inconvenienced by having to share space with sawhorses and paint buckets and drop cloths. "Remember, it's only for the summer."

6

Suddenly Becka's sunny pastel-colored dream-come-true summer darkened into a stormy rain-drenched nightmare named . . .

Marianne.

She arrived last night from the airport. It was dinnertime, but Marianne said she was too tired to eat, and asked if it would be OK to go straight to bed.

Becka's mother smiled and got up to ready the bed in Becka's room.

Marianne looked alarmed. "No," she said anxiously, "I'll do it."

Becka watched her carry the sheets and blanket upstairs. But on the landing Marianne stopped momentarily, her foot above the stair tread. She turned and looked back at Becka and grinned. It gave Becka a chill.

That night Becka phoned all her friends but only got their answering machines. *Strange,* she thought, *were they all out together?* She felt panicky. What if they had seen her with Marianne? What if they no longer wanted her in The Group?

The rain began early the next morning and continued throughout the day. Becka took Marianne to the mall to look for new shoes. She told her mother she wanted to go to the Mission Hills Mall.

"But that's so far away."

Becka shrugged. The truth was she didn't want to go anywhere her friends might see her with Marianne.

The mall was pretty crowded. They poked around a bunch of shops and then had lunch. Becka had a yogurt with granola and a cookie. Marianne had some rice and chicken. As they got up to leave, Becka noticed that

Marianne had hardly eaten any of her lunch. She had swept it up quickly and dropped the carton into the trash.

"Not hungry?"

Marianne shook her head and smiled wanly.

What a weirdo, thought Becka.

BECKA HAD STRANGE dreams throughout the night. When she woke up the next morning she felt vaguely uneasy. It was as if someone had been watching her through her bedroom window.

Marianne was already awake. The guest bed was made. Becka looked out the window. It had stopped raining; the sun was shining and the sky was a brilliant deep blue.

She could hear the hissing of the shower in the bathroom down the hall.

She took a few steps across the carpet and yelped, pulling herself up on her toes. The carpet was sopping wet! A damp trail of footprints led from the guest bed out the door. Footprints crusted with sand.

Becka thought, *Marianne?*

She tiptoed down the hall to the bathroom. The door was closed, and she tapped lightly. "Marianne? Marianne, are you in there?" She was just about to knock again when the door opened a few inches from the inside. The air was foggy with steam. The shower was hissing at full blast.

"Marianne?" said Becka, fanning away the steam with her hands.

A voice behind her whispered, "Here I am."

Becka whirled and screamed. "Ah! Marianne, you scared me to death. What's your problem, sneaking up behind me like that? And why is the water still running? Don't you know there is, like, a water shortage?"

Marianne stared at her, unblinking. Then she smiled. It was a smile that pulled sideways across her teeth like a slash and didn't curl up at the ends. Her jet black hair was parted in the middle and hung in long damp strands over her face. She stared at Becka through black eyes as flat and hard as polished marble.

"Did you go to the beach this morning?" asked Becka.

"No."

Becka cocked one hip and put a finger to her lips. She affected a sarcastic tone. Sarcasm was the weapon of choice among members of The Group. "Really? Gee, I wonder how come there are soggy sandy footprints on the carpet? Hmmmm."

Marianne shrugged.

Becka flung open the door of the shower. Swatting at a cloud of steam, she turned to Marianne accusingly.

"Explain this."

The tiles were covered with swirling eddies of sand, and tangled threads of seaweed clogged the drain.

Marianne's cold grin deepened, and Becka suddenly felt herself on the defensive. An unpleasant aroma like hot sour breath caressed her face and made her stomach roll unsteadily.

Marianne finally broke off her gaze, turned sideways, and slipped passed Becka.

Becka showered and put on her favorite new bathing suit and slipped on a pair of baggy shorts and a cropped T-shirt. The she went downstairs for breakfast.

Marianne was reading a book and sipping a cup of tea. She was tall, and thin as a pole. Her shaggy black hair had been pulled through a bright red-and-white scrunchie. Her long skinny arms and legs reminded Becka of an insect's. Her skin was pale blue, like milk. Under each eye were dark crescents.

"What are you reading?" asked Becka.

"*Crime and Punishment*. Dostoevsky."

"Sounds boring," Becka shrugged. She watched Marianne slowly turn a page in her book. She reminded Becka of a corpse. *I can even see her veins.*

Her mother came out of the kitchen with bowls of fruit and cereal.

"Nothing for me," said Marianne. "I don't like to eat."

Becka dropped her spoon. "What do you mean you don't like to eat? Everybody eats. What are you, some kind of vampire or something?"

Her mother glared at her. "What your cousin means is, she's not hungry." Then she turned to Marianne. "But you really should eat something, Marianne. You've hardly eaten since you've been here. It isn't my cooking, is it? Because if there is something special you want, that's no problem."

Marianne said, "Maybe a piece of toast." She smiled sweetly.

Becka tried calling her friends. But once again all she could do was leave messages on their machines. She was coming out of the family room when she bumped into

11

Marianne, who was wearing a beautiful necklace with a tear drop pearl pendant.

"Where did you get that?"

Marianne fingered the pearl absently, then said, "I got it at the mall, when you were busy making phone calls. Do you like it?"

Becka narrowed her eyes. "I guess. It looks like a pearl necklace that belongs to my best friend, Monica."

"What are you suggesting?"

Becka shook her head, "Nothing."

Later Becka was talking with her mother in the laundry room. They were downstairs in the basement. The air was warm and smelled of soap.

"Help me fold these," her mother said, bundling some towels from the dryer. "Your cousin is from Iowa. I guess they do things differently there."

"I'll say."

Her mother frowned at Becka. "Be nice to her. Marianne doesn't make friends easily. She's very shy." Her mother looked away and then let out her breath. "Apparently Marianne has a few . . . problems."

Becka snorted. "No kidding. The girl is a total nut job."

"She's a perfectly sweet girl."

Becka shot her a you-must-be-kidding glance. "What about the not eating thing?"

"She's self-conscious about her figure."

"What figure? She doesn't have a figure. She doesn't sleep either."

"Not everyone needs sixteen hours of sleep, Becka." Her mother looked at her reprovingly, then turned away.

"She smells. I mean she really smells. She stinks like dead fish and old seaweed."

"That's enough, young lady."

"But she does! It's, like, totally gross."

"I said *enough*. For the last week I've endured your constant whining and complaining, and I'm sick of it. OK? Beginning right now you'll start treating Marianne as a guest in this house. And I mean you will be on your absolute best behavior. Or else. Do you understand me?"

The next day Marianne found Becka sitting on the front porch.

"You want to go to the beach?" asked Marianne. She had a different scrunchie on this morning. Becka thought it looked familiar. Then she realized it was exactly the same one that she had given Alicia for her birthday.

"OK."

It was a short walk to the beach. They reached the crest of a fenced bluff, then walked down a steep path that wound through a canyon.

Along the way, Marianne turned to Becka.

"I'm sorry about all this. I know my coming here has ruined your summer. And I completely understand how bad it must be for you. I've ruined everything for you. Believe me, I know what it's like not to be able to hang out with friends. I don't blame you for hating me."

Becka was stunned. "It's not like I *hate* you, exactly."

Marianne nodded, "It's OK. I was just hoping that we might be friends."

Before Becka had a chance to take it back, she said, "OK."

The sky was overcast, and the glare of the sun turned the sea into a polished sheet of metal. The beach was deserted except for a few mothers and their kids camped under umbrellas that sprouted in the sand like rainbow-colored mushrooms.

A boy with a surfboard walking along the edge of the beach called out to Becka. She smiled and waved. It was Matt. Another boy came loping out of the surf behind Matt and joined him. Derrick Matthews.

"Wait here," Becka said coldly to Marianne. Then she walked over to talk with Matt and Derrick.

"Hey, Becka. Where've you been? And who's the ghoul?" asked Matt.

"My creepy cousin. That's how come I haven't been around."

"Totally Morticia Adams," joked Derrick.

"No kidding. Hey, have you guys seen Alicia and Monica?"

Matt shook his head. "I thought they were with you."

"What about LizBeth?"

Matt shrugged.

Becka frowned. "OK. Well, if you see them, tell them I'm baby-sitting The Ghoul."

Derrick asked, "Hey, you're not heading up toward Miller's Point, are you?"

Becka frowned. The truth was, Becka didn't want to risk her reputation by being seen with a loser like Marianne, even if it meant walking all the way to

Miller's Point, where she was pretty sure they would be alone.

"I don't know. Maybe."

Matt narrowed his eyes. "But what about that girl who—you know . . ."

Becka sighed. "Look, that story is just a myth. That girl didn't kill herself off the point. It never happened. She was, like, a total emotional wreck. I heard she was sent away to some special school somewhere. Anyway, I gotta go." She shrugged her shoulders, smiled coyly at Matt, and walked back to Marianne.

They walked along the water's edge to where the beach made a wide curve. At the far end of the curve a tumble of huge rocks jutted out into the sea. Miller's Point.

"Tell me about the girl who killed herself," said Marianne.

Becka stopped dead in her tracks. Her eyes narrowed suspiciously. "Who told you about her? What do you know about it?"

Marianne shrugged, but Becka saw in her eyes a glint of triumph. "I just heard things. From kids in the neighborhood."

"You don't know any kids in the neighborhood."

Marianne sniffed haughtily. "It's just a story, right, Becka? It's not like you had anything to do with it."

"That's right. I didn't even really know the kid. She was in my class in fifth grade. I mean it's not like we were friends or anything."

They walked a long way. After a while the smooth sand turned pebbly and rough with rocks and boulders.

Becka had never come this far up shore. At least, not since the girl's body had been discovered drowned in a pool by the rocks. Becka tried to forget, but that only made the memory more real. It was a harmless prank. Kids' stuff.

Becka couldn't even remember the girl's name.

All Becka could remember was that the girl didn't have any friends at all. Even The Untouchables shunned her. And they were so unpopular they would accept just about anyone.

But ever since the accident, the rocks at Miller's Point had become a kind of weird shrine to the girl's memory.

"This is far enough," said Becka. She threw down her pack, flipped out her blanket, and lay down. Marianne sat next to her in the sand. Becka couldn't believe that she didn't burn in the sun. Her skin was as white as cream.

Becka sat up, startled. "What did you say?"

Marianne squinted at her as she let a handful of sand run idly through her fingers. "Nothing, Becka. Go back to sleep."

Becka let out a long sighing breath.

The sun was coming out from behind the haze and it felt exhilarating on Becka's skin. She had the portable radio tuned to her favorite station. All she needed was her real friends and it would be a perfect day. She tried to concentrate on forgetting about Marianne. After a while she squinted her eyes and peeked sideways at Marianne. Marianne had her knees pulled up, and her chin rested on her folded arms.

Becka shivered.

After a while the sun was making her drowsy, and before long the low drumming of the waves crowded out thoughts of Marianne, and Becka fell into a deep sleep.

She was awakened by a voice calling her name.

Becka sat up. The sand and sky were a ferocious white glare that stung her eyes. It took some time for them to adjust. *Where was Marianne?* She looked up and down the beach but saw no one.

Becka!

Becka corkscrewed one way. "Monica?" And then the other. "Alicia, where are you?" There was no one on the beach, but she heard her friends' voices calling her. *Where are they?* Becka walked down to the water's edge.

There she spun around and around. "Where are you?" An edge of panic crept into her voice. "Come on, you guys, this isn't funny! Tell me where you are!" She noticed a trail of footprints in the sand that lead along the beach to where the massive rock arch of Miller's Point jutted out into the sea.

"Monica?" she called out tentatively.

Becka, we're down here . . .

Reluctantly Becka slogged through the shallow sea water and climbed out onto the rocks. She stood up unsteadily and gazed down at the waves that looped and curled around the rocks. A swelling gust of wind rushed across the jagged rocks and clutched at her. She felt wobbly and had to steady herself with outstretched arms.

"Alicia? Monica?"

Becka was standing in front of a dark hollow formed by two rock slabs that tilted head to head. She nervously peered down into the hollow. It seemed to drop steeply, then stop and curve inward. Vaguely she could hear the muffled rumbling of waves sloshing back and forth inside.

We're in here.

Becka crouched and peered down. "Where? Where are you?"

A voice from behind made Becka whirl and scream.

"Here we are." It was Marianne. Her lips were stretched in a snarl. Becka was so frightened that she lost her footing and fell headlong down the mouth of the tunnel. Her head cracked hard on the rock.

When she regained consciousness she was staring up into the dome of an underwater cavern. Water misted on the ceiling and rained down in a steady rhythm. She slid up into a sitting position and dabbed the back of her head. A whispering voice rose like mist over the pool of water.

Becka looked up.

Marianne was backed up against the wall of rock, staring at her.

"What?" Becka heard herself ask groggily. The pungent stink of brackish water and rotting fish made her wince, and she thought she might vomit.

"I said, 'Nice of you to drop in.'"

Becka sobbed, "Is that supposed to be a joke?"

"Yes!" Marianne nodded thoughtfully. She stood up and walked over to Becka. Marianne gave her cousin a can-you-keep-a-secret grin, then whispered: "Maybe you would like to hear a little story?"

Becka shook her head, no. "That's too bad, because this is a really good story. And best of all, it's true. Once upon a time, there was a little girl who wanted to be popular. But none of the other girls liked her. They teased her and told her she was ugly and wouldn't let her play with them. And they wouldn't let other little girls play with her either. So the poor little girl had no friends at all."

Becka looked at Marianne and swallowed. It was like seeing an apparition in the fog slowly coming into focus.

"But that wasn't the worst of it. One day the popular girls thought it would be hilariously funny to play a trick on the poor little girl. They pretended they wanted to be friends with her. They even invited her to the beach. But the little girl had not grown up near the sea. She didn't know how to swim. 'That's okay,' they said. 'We'll teach you.' And the little girl believed them. Because that's how much she wanted to have friends."

Becka slowly shook her head. "No way."

"Yes, way. But the girls didn't want to teach her how to swim, did they Becka. No, they wanted to humiliate her. So they pushed her underwater. And every time she struggled and gasped, they would push her down again. And all the time they did this, the girls laughed and laughed and laughed."

Becka pleaded, "It was just a stupid prank. You were OK. You didn't drown. I saw you run away."

Marianne sneered.

The tide inside the cavern was rising. It had climbed up as high as Becka's knees and was rising steadily. She could feel the heavy sloshing of the water as the waves surged underground and erupted up into the cavern. "What are you going to do?"

Marianne appeared to have ignored her question. Her eyes lost all focus and seemed to draw inward toward some long-forgotten memory. "It's all right now, though. The little girl found a way to be friends with them after all."

"What are you talking about? What friends? Who are you?"

Becka frantically worked her way along the wall, fingers splayed against the barnacled rock, all the while the sea water continuing to rise. There must be a way out! The sea water was past her waist now.

"You're crazy," Becka screamed. "That's what you are! You ought to be locked up! I hate you! You hear me? I hate you!"

Marianne sighed. "That's no way to talk to your best friend, Becks."

"I'm not your friend," Becka snarled. Suddenly she felt something against her leg. She jumped sideways through the water. A hand reached around her ankle. It tightened and tried to pull her down!

"No!" Something coiled around her wrist. Frantic, she looked down. Another hand had emerged from the water. The fingers encircling her wrist were white as ivory and bloated as an inflated rubber glove. Becka screamed.

We're all here now, Becka.

Becka felt the breath leave her suddenly. Terror buckled her knees as another hand pushed up through the water. And another. And another. Bloated fingers reached for her. Clawed at her. She tried to dodge them, but it was no use. Suddenly an arm emerged from the water.

Becka tried to scream. But as the head of her best friend, Monica, bobbed to the surface—its features distorted like those of a hideous Halloween pumpkin—her words caught in her throat.

A second head rose from the depths. Becka felt the tears rolling down her face.

"Oh my," she whimpered. "Alicia!"

The sea water continued to rise. It climbed up just below Becka's neck.

Marianne sighed happily. "Don't worry, Becka. It won't hurt . . . much."

"You won't get away with this," sputtered Becka. The sea water was closing over her mouth. With her arms pinned to her sides she could not keep her head above water. Her friends were holding her down.

Marianne grinned.

"I told you I found a way we could all be friends."

WHEN MARIANNE GOT back to the house she saw a very pretty girl standing impatiently on the front porch. "Who are you?" she asked.

The girl turned and gave Marianne a chilly once-over. "Isn't it a little early for Halloween?"

"I'm Becka's cousin, Marianne."

The girl cocked a hip. "Great. Where's Becka?"

Marianne turned and looked back over her shoulder, then at the girl. "You must be LizBeth."

The girl glared at Marianne. "Yeah. So? Where's Becka?"

"She and the rest of The Group are waiting for you down at Miller's Point."

"How do you know about The Group?"

Marianne smiled. "Oh, I know all about The Group." She gestured for LizBeth to follow.

THE DARE

I **HEARD ABOUT THIS** spot even before my family up
and moved from San Diego. It was reported to be an
excellent right break. Storms originating off the Aleutian
Islands in Alaska roared down the coast, and as they
drove south they picked up speed and strength. Then
they smacked head-on into a bluff that jutted about a
half-mile off shore. It was like throwing the brakes on a
runaway locomotive. All of a sudden, tons of water came
heaving forward.

It was a right break, and very steep. A *cannonball* right.

I watched the waves for a while, taking notes in my
mind and making adjustments. Just like a coach going over
tapes of last night's game.

Think of yourself as the quarterback. The sea is the
hulking defensive back across the line, with missing teeth

and twin jets of steam blowing out his nose, like the stampeding bull in cartoons.

Underestimate him and you'll end up singing in the choir.

People don't realize how dangerous surfing can be. And it isn't just falling on your board or being hit in the head or other obvious hazards. It's all the other stuff. Currents so strong they could pull a freight train off its tracks. And riptides and undertows. I've seen rips that could suck the pit out of a cherry.

This break is called Zeroes. I don't know why, but I figure it must have something to do with some local legend. Most breaks have names that are like some kind of code. It's a way locals have of keeping out nonlocals. Like me.

The beach is only a short bike ride from our house. That was one cool thing about moving to Santa Cruz. Now I could surf every morning, no problem. Morning was coming on fast. The sun climbed higher. The sky turned from a dark blue and green to a light powdery blue. I could make out the waves easily, rolling toward shore in long columns like a marching band.

They hadn't lied about this being a hellacious break.

The waves were big and powerful and pulled a lot of water and looked very fast. I scanned for an escape channel—something that looked like an oily ribbon out past the breakers. The last thing I need was to get caught inside the rough water and be smashed against the cliff rocks.

I found the channel, no problem.

Off to the left about a hundred yards away was a huge flat rock. It was home to a colony of seals. Barking like crazy, they were slipping in and out of the water around the rock.

I had surfed with dolphins and porpoises before. Lots of times. But never seals.

I rolled my shoulders to work out the kinks. I started to stand up when some kid my age ran by and yelled, "Hey! Princess! You snooze, you lose."

I spun around. The jerk had surprised me. My foot slipped on a slick rock, and I tumbled and fell. My CD player smashed on the rocks, and I must have cursed because as the jerk ran by he laughed, shaking his head.

He danced over the rocks, his surfboard tucked under his arm. About knee-high in the water, he slung the board under him with a stiff-arm motion and began paddling. Then he twisted his head around to toss a smirk my way.

It was a total in-your-face challenge. Local to an outsider. It said: Stay off my beach.

I paddled out after him. When I hit the water it felt like I had just dived into a bucket of ice. My breath caught in my chest, and I had to pry my jaw open with my tongue.

The kid looked over his shoulder again. I saw him shake his head. I paddled hard in the kid's wake. We headed straight out to sea, then made a hard right and angled toward the break.

The kid quit paddling and sat straddling his board. As I came up behind him, he totally ignored me and sat bobbing in the water, face to the horizon, the nose of his board angled up.

The smart thing would have been to position myself behind him. Closer to shore. Let the local have the first wave. Take the second. It would be bigger anyway. But I was angry at being slighted. This guy was treating me like I was some kind of amateur.

You want the real story, I was *ranked*. I'd been surfing the junior circuit in Southern California for years. My room was crammed with trophies I'd won. I was even thinking about turning pro some day. So where did this punk get off giving me the smirk shoulder?

OK, bring it on.

The kid suddenly leaned forward, brought the board up under him, and paddled hard. A big comber was rolling toward us. I took a few deep strokes and came up next to him. The kid glared, "My wave!"

I smiled. Suddenly both of us rose with the face of the wave. It was a big wave. Big and sleek with a deep slide. Maybe seven, eight feet. The kid jumped to his feet and planted.

I hesitated just a second. But that was too long. The wave peaked and caught me in midair. I was caught out of position. Instead of planting my feet firmly on the board, I was in free fall. The board skipped out from under me and twirled in the air. I hit the water hard.

It felt as if I'd been dropped onto a concrete sidewalk. The wind was knocked out of me.

I popped to the surface just as another wave crashed down on my head. I was dragged down. The water, churning like the inside of a washing machine, turned me upside down. When I finally clawed my way to the surface, I was out of breath and panicky. I felt like a total loser.

I was coughing and spluttering, and my hair was plastered over my face. I heard the jerk laughing his head off.

"Hey, Princess! Try the granny break down the beach!"

I looked for my board. It was almost all the way in toward shore. And broken nearly in half. I couldn't believe it. There was no way the wave came down that hard.

My first day at Zeroes had been just that: a zero.

I grabbed my stuff and found my bike and rode home. The board was a total loss. I was about to heave it into the trash when I noticed something embedded in the fiberglass along the edge of the break. I found a screwdriver in the garage and pried that something out.

It was triangular in shape. About three inches high, with a serrated edge on two sides. I didn't need a dictionary to tell me what it meant: "shark tooth."

The next day at school I just kind of happened to mention my discovery. I tried to make it sound like no big deal. The thing is, I really didn't have any friends yet, so I was fair game for any wise guy who wanted to take a shot.

I was standing outside my math class. A group of kids huddled around me. One of them I kind of knew: Eric. He was a surfer.

Just my luck that Jerk Boy happened to stroll by at that moment. Turns out his name was Hunter. Right away most of the other kids walked over to him. He stopped and gave me the once-over. He and Eric just happened to be the best of friends.

I heard them talking, and then Hunter flipped his chin toward me. Suddenly all the kids started to laugh.

Hunter walked up to me. "You afraid of a shark?"

"No way."

He grinned over his shoulder at Eric, then back at me.

"Prove it, Princess. Meet me tomorrow. You know where." Then he walked off. Not sure of what I'd gotten myself into, I leaned back against my locker, feeling as if I'd wandered into a nightmare episode of *Saved by the Bell*.

The next morning I was on the beach, waxing my replacement board. For some reason, I expected Hunter to come strolling down the beach, followed by a crowd armed with chains and tire jacks.

But it was just him.

He barely cut a glance in my direction, then paddled out.

I tried to act cool.

I cut Jerk Boy some slack and stayed out of his way. No sense butting heads. But Hunter was not the only thing on my mind. I kept thinking about the shark. I'd seen enough PBS specials to know that sharks don't hunt humans. Of course, that's what they always say just before they show you a totally barfish photo of some guy with his leg sawed off at the knee.

The waves picked up, and my mind cleared.

Hunter caught the first wave. I waited a few times, then did the same. This time I handled the drop much better. I made my turn a little too steeply but compensated with a neat off the shoulder that sent a rooster tail of white water into the air. Hunter paddled back, and I saw him actually nod appreciatively.

Next time out I would do the same.

The truth is Hunter could really surf. He was tall and loose-limbed and moved so smoothly that the board seemed like an extension of his arms and legs.

29

The rest of the morning we exchanged waves. We weren't buddies yet. Jerk Boy still kept mostly to himself. No conversation. No ribbing. But I respected his ability. And I think he had come to respect mine.

Maybe not. By this time I really didn't care. I was back. I was enjoying myself surfing. I hadn't felt that rush and exhilaration in a long time. Santa Cruz might not be such a bad place after all.

I was almost ready to pack it in when I saw Hunter drop down into a huge wave. It was easily the wave of the day, ten maybe twelve feet. He made a slashing bottom turn and kicked into a rebound off the lip. I could see the long arcing rainbow in the spray. It was a monster move.

Say what you will: The guy was awesome.

I paddled out and waited for the last wave. The wind was already shifting on shore. The next few waves mushed, and I took a pass. I was paddling back to shore when it occurred to me that Hunter had not paddled back out. I couldn't see him anywhere. I ran my eyes up and down along the shoreline. Weird.

That's when I saw his board floating midway between me and the shore. I looked left and right. Nothing. I paddled after the board.

A feeling of dread coursed through my body as I approached the board: It had been bitten in half. On one half I could clearly see the outline of a very large jaw. My heart was pounding. Just then I saw Hunter about ten yards away. His eyes were white and lifeless. He was partly submerged in the kelp and was rolled onto his back. The water around him was stained red.

I pulled my legs out of the water, then my arms. Stay calm, I told myself. I scanned the water around me, but there was nothing—no huge fin slicing through the surface, no dark shadow gliding toward me from the deep.

My heart was hammering like a hydraulic jack. I couldn't breathe. I kept blowing air out in big chunks but couldn't get any in.

And I couldn't rip my eyes away from Hunter's body bobbing in front of me in a pool of blood. My mind was spinning. I clung to one thought: Sharks don't eat humans, at least, not on purpose . . . right?

I had to do something, but I didn't know what. I started swimming toward Hunter when the water around me exploded. A huge jaw rimmed with razor-sharp teeth lunged from the water. It was heading right for me. More out of fright than anything, I slid off my board just as the shark's jaw clamped down. I heard a crunch. The shark snapped his head back and forth.

My mind was a blur as I reached Hunter and looped my arms under his. Luckily his wet suit was keeping him afloat.

In my panic I figured if I could dog-paddle us to the rock, we might be safe. It was only about fifteen yards away.

I remember shouting at Hunter. Screaming encouragement. "You can do it! C'mon! We're almost there!"

A wave rolled over us and pushed us down. I clamped a hand over his nose and mouth. I was afraid he might inhale some water and drown. Then when I broke to the surface I breathed too soon and sucked in a mouthful of salt water.

The whole time I kept wondering: *Where is he? Where is the shark?*

"C'mon. You can make it!" The big flat rock hung just out of reach.

Just then I felt something brush under my feet.

"Oh, my—" I was ten yards from the rock. But it seemed like a million miles away. This time as the shark circled under me it bumped me hard. Instinctively I froze and pulled my legs up. Between me and the rock a fin rose up out of the water as the shark rolled slightly to one side and showed me its dull black eye.

Then, about fifteen yards to my left, the shark's dorsal fin broke the surface. It was heading right for us. I froze. It was dumb luck that the shark came to a sudden stop about five yards in front of us.

The jaw snapped and the head twisted sideways. I saw the black eye rolling in its socket. The jaws kept opening and closing. What was going on?

Suddenly I realized the shark hadn't missed us at all. It might not even have been chasing us. It had caught a seal. What I had thought was blind frenzied snapping was actually the shark devouring its victim.

Still dragging Hunter, I clawed backward among the shallow rocks, fumbling for solid footing. I caught hold and hauled myself up into a standing position. I then heaved Hunter onto the rocks. The shark had torn a dreadfully large chunk of flesh from his thigh. But considering how easily it had disposed of the seal, I figured Hunter had to consider himself lucky. He had lost a lot of blood, though. I figured he was in shock, but I wasn't sure how much blood a body could lose before it was too late. I removed the top of his wet suit and listened for a heartbeat.

Yes!

It was faint. No more than a tiny blip. But it was there.

I knew I had to get help, and fast. I had to swim to shore. My hope was that the shark was too busy bobbing for seal to be interested in making me its next meal. I stripped off my wet suit. The heavy neoprene would slow me down. I bundled up the wet suit and slipped it under Hunter's head.

I stood there shivering. The water was black and cold and somewhere down there a killer shark hunted. My courage vanished.

I can't, I thought. I took a deep breath.

"I can." I said it again: "I can!" Then I dived into the water and swam as fast as I could for shore.

HUNTER HAD HIS LEG in a cast. "I guess I won't be surfing for awhile."

His best friend, Eric, said, "I'm surprised you still want to. After what happened."

"Are you insane? The minute this cast comes off, I'm out there!" He turned toward me. "What about you, Princess?"

I laughed. The kid was totally nuts. Even after everything he had been through, all he could think about was surfing. I said, "If you go, I guess I'll have to go."

Hunter narrowed his eyes and smirked. "Yeah, who else am I going to show up so bad?"

I grinned. "You mean, who else is going to carry you back to shore?"

Hunter smiled and limped away.

EYES

THE DOORBELL RANG. Rachel listened to the screen door swing open, then slap shut. Next came steps on the stairs, then on the landing. Now coming down the hall. Followed by a light tapping on her bedroom door.

"Rachel, honey? It's me. Mom." The door was pushed open a crack.

"Go away."

The head withdrew, like a turtle's into its shell. "Aaron is downstairs. He wants to see you."

"Tell him to go away."

Rachel's mom pushed the bedroom door shut. Her footsteps trailing away were hurried.

The accident had been six months ago. A cold and drizzly January afternoon. Rachel was in the backseat of a taxi, on the way home from the train station, when a sports utility vehicle broadsided them. The taxi driver escaped without injury. Rachel wasn't so fortunate.

Aaron came to see her in the hospital one afternoon after school. She turned him away then too. And mostly everybody else who came to see her. After a while Rachel recovered. Her bruises healed. Her cuts healed. Everything felt like normal—except her eyes. The doctors said they would never heal. Otherwise she looked normal. On the outside.

Aaron came again the next afternoon. And the next. And every day after that. He would knock on her door and politely ask to come in. He joked with her through the door and talked in funny cartoon voices and waited patiently for her to laugh. Each time Rachel told him to go home.

He left her presents by the door—CDs by her favorite groups, books on tape . . . stuff like that. When he returned the next day, the presents would be sitting outside the door, waiting for her mother to scoop them up and put them in a box down in the basement.

Summer was on its way. The days were growing longer and warmer. School would be over soon. Rachel supposed Aaron would be prepping his day sailor. He'd be in his backyard, cleaning and repainting the hull of his Sunfish. Rachel saw the boat in her mind.

Aaron liked to sail just as much as Rachel did. And he was a pretty good sailor. He had a thorough knowledge of the sea. But more often than not, he was content to keep his boat trimmed close to shore, lacking the nerve to venture boldly into open water.

Not like Rachel. Rachel had a gift. She was like a bird on the wing: natural and free, gliding on the water as if sailing through the sky. She had an instinct for the water, and she was fearless. But she was not reckless. Rachel had nothing but contempt for inexperienced sailors who tested themselves by attempting more than they should.

Rachel was more at home on the water than on land.

The accident changed everything.

The first day home from the hospital she had stripped all her sailing posters from her bedroom walls. The dozens of trophies Rachel had won in junior races over the years she hid away in boxes in the basement. She hardly ever left her bedroom anymore.

One day Rachel heard Aaron and her mother talking outside the front door. They usually spoke for a few minutes before Aaron left, but today was unusual because Rachel couldn't hear what they were saying. Their whispers didn't reach her second-story window.

Rachel heard Aaron pedaling away on his bicycle. She stood alone at her bedroom window, the sun on her face. A breeze fluttered the curtains, and she smelled the sea. A sudden grief stabbed her. It was all a cruel reminder of a beautiful world that had vanished forever.

She slammed the window shut.

The next day Rachel had a doctor's appointment. She and her mom drove past the harbor on the way into town. Gulls cried and wheeled overhead. Rachel turned her face to the open window and listened to the snap of the halyards. Giant expanses of sail luffed in the breeze and bellied out as skippers made sail. Beyond the sea break the deep-blue sea beckoned. It was the kind of day that used to make Rachel giddy with anticipation.

But today Rachel rolled up the window hastily and snapped on the radio. She hunched down low in her seat.

"What's the matter?" her mother asked.

"I wish I were dead." Rachel said matter-of-factly.

Her mother tried to sound casual. "Dr. Henderson wants to perform a new test today."

"What kind of test?" Rachel asked suspiciously.

Her mother shrugged and answered breezily, "It's something new, honey." Up ahead she spied Aaron at the side of the road. Behind him sailboats bobbed lazily in the harbor. The car pulled to the side of the road and stopped. The passenger door was pulled open.

"What's going on?" demanded Rachel.

"It's me," said Aaron.

"Aaron? What are you doing here? What's going on?"

Aaron lifted Rachel out of the car. She had put on weight, and Aaron staggered before regaining his balance. "We're going for a ride," he huffed.

"Put me down!" shrieked Rachel. She kicked and flailed her arms. "Mom," she yelled. But the car had sped away.

Aaron plonked her down in a shopping cart he had "borrowed" from the local Safeway™. Aaron began wheeling the cart down the sidewalk toward the dock.

"Help!" she shouted. Rachel felt like an upended tortoise. She was all scrunched up like a folding chair, and her knees drummed on her shoulders as the cart bumped over the timbered dock. Aaron pushed the cart faster and faster.

"Almost there!" shouted Aaron as the cart hit the inclined ramp that led to the boat launch.

"Stop!" screamed Rachel.

"Hold on!" yelled Aaron. The cart shimmied and began to turn sideways. At the last second he dragged the cart to an abrupt stop. It tipped forward, and Rachel was dumped unceremoniously onto the wooden dock like a sack of potatoes.

"Er . . . sorry," Aaron apologized.

"Take me home."

"Can't do that." He took her by the hand. "There's something I want you to see."

She yanked away her hand. Aaron cringed. "Sorry . . . again." He half led, half pulled her to a small sailboat moored sideways to the dock. He jumped in amidships and reached up for Rachel. "C'mon."

"I can't." She was shaking her head.

"Yes, you can."

"I can't!"

Aaron spoke crossly. "Yes, you can, Rachel. Now c'mon. Either you climb in on your own, or I'll carry you in myself." He reached out his hand and added gently, "Please."

A paralyzing panic made her breathless. Rachel was so angry with Aaron and her mom for tricking her that she wanted to scream. And she felt so hopeless and lost that she wanted to cry. Most of all she wanted someone to throw their arms around her and tell her it had all been just a bad dream. The accident. The blindness.

But she knew it was no dream.

She reached out with a trembling hand. Her fingers grabbed at empty air. "Where are you?" she whimpered. Her fingers caught hold of his and coiled tight.

"I'm here, Rachel."

She stepped down into the boat. It felt as if the earth were turning and tossing under her. Not at all like she remembered. She had always been so sure footed on the water. "I can't do this."

"Yes, you can," said Aaron.

Rachel swallowed hard, her legs trembling. Aaron took her by the hand and brought her to the back of the boat and sat her down.

"Put this on."

She threw it back at him. Again he plunked the life jacket in her lap. "Put it on."

Aaron worked methodically. He pushed the boat away from the dock and rowed to open water. He hoisted the mainsail, then the jib. Once the sails were properly trimmed, he lowered the centerboard halfway and gently pushed away on the rudder. A light but steady breeze bellied the sails, and the boat headed out of the channel.

Once clear of the harbor, Aaron dropped the centerboard full.

"How do you feel?"

Rachel was hunched in the stern, her knees up and arms crossed tightly. "I want to go home now."

"No."

Aaron inhaled deeply and let his thoughts wander.

The sky was a brilliant icy blue, with only a few bundles of cumulus clouds on the horizon. Aaron pulled in on the rudder and lightly adjusted the mainsheet. He squinted up the mast at the telltale, a length of ribbon attached near the top of the mainsail that helped to gauge the trim on the sails.

He nodded, pleased with himself.

"You're pinched," Rachel grumbled.

"No way." Suddenly the sail started to flutter and whip about. Aaron realized he was trimmed too tight. He cursed under his breath and corrected.

Rachel smirked. "Told you so."

Aaron smiled secretly inside. It was a start.

Rachel had dreaded this moment more than anything. She felt like someone who'd wandered out onto a thin sheet of ice—pleased to be standing but uncertain how long that would last. Since the accident, she had tried to erase every pleasant memory from her past. She didn't want anything to be the same as before, even if that meant pushing away everything she loved. And everyone.

But she couldn't stop the wind in her hair and the salt water misting her face from bringing on a rush of wonderful memories. She closed her eyes and saw herself sailing. The sky was pale blue, and the sea sparkled. Staring up at the sky, she saw the sun as a smudged blur of bright white through her sails, brilliant and dazzling. She was flying: lost in the air and skating on the wind. She wasn't at all certain she wanted to forget this feeling.

Without thinking, she opened her eyes. A dark veil pulled itself across the sun and blotted out the sky. She was in darkness. She cursed herself for letting down her guard.

A drop of rain plopped on her cheek. Then another. Rachel perked up suddenly. "Aaron!"

Aaron had been caught drowsing at the tiller. "What's the matter?" he asked groggily.

"Tell me where the clouds are." Aaron gazed toward the horizon, embarrassed to be caught off guard. He said offhandedly, "Starboard." Suddenly Aaron was nervous. The fluffy white clouds had gathered into a broiling thunderhead on the horizon.

A handful of raindrops pelted Rachel's face and shoulders. She felt a sudden rush of anxiety. "Jibe," she said.

"What?" Aaron sat up straight. In his hand, the tiller suddenly began to shake violently.

"Rachel, it's OK. There really isn't any reason . . ."

"Jibe!"

But it was too late. As Aaron guided the boat on its tack from port to starboard, the gentle breeze suddenly galed. A violent eruption of wind tore into the sail. Aaron tried to duck. But the boom swung too fast and sidearmed him in the back of the head. There was a loud THUNK, and Aaron crumpled to the deck as the tiller swung free.

"Aaron!" screamed Rachel. "Aaron! Are you all right?"

Her brain was a jumble. In the shrieking wind, the sheets rumpled and snapped. She scrambled crablike over to Aaron and found him slumped on his side. Panic seized her. Her hands fumbled over him and felt behind his head. He was bleeding. A large knot as big as her fist had already formed. The boat heaved suddenly. Rachel fell back, and her shoulder landed hard against the tiller mount.

The mainsail was flapping and fluttering. The boat pitched again and made a groaning half turn. Rachel was again knocked against the gunwale. A stabbing pain ripped through her side.

She took a deep breath. The boat was bobbing in a freak wind, with no sailor at the tiller. She had to correct that. But first she had to see to Aaron.

Please be OK!

She crawled over to him, her bruised arm tucked protectively against her left side.

"Aaron?" She ran a hand over him. He was lying facedown now. "Aaron?" She found an arm and thumbed for a pulse. A wave of relief washed over her when she felt the faint but unmistakable beating. She wrestled herself out of her life jacket, pulled off her sweatshirt, and balled it up under his head.

The boat suddenly dipped, then heeled and lurched to the leeward. The lurching sent Rachel sprawling sideways. She was being flung overboard! But just then, her right hand dragged over a cleat and she grabbed hold of it just in time.

The cold water was like an electric shock. Frantically, she hooked her right arm around the cleat and pulled herself up.

She was in the boat.

She collapsed hard on her side. The pain was unbearable. Her hands were shaking, and her legs felt like two blocks of cement.

"What am I supposed to do? I can't see."

The wind howled, and again the boat heeled over. The starboard gunwale was below water. Rachel clutched a cleat to keep from slipping overboard a second time as a gust of spray slapped her face. She was ready to quit. She didn't care if she drowned. Isn't that what she had wished for all these months? To be dead? She decided to give up, to jump overboard. She pictured herself sinking slowly to the bottom. It was so quiet down there. Peaceful. It would be so easy . . .

But then she thought about Aaron, and she couldn't do it. She took a few deep breaths.

Think! she told herself. *Think! Think! Think!*

The first thing to do was dump some wind from the sails. *Reefing.* That would keep the boat from capsizing: Less sail meant less wind in the sail. She scrambled to the mast and fumbled for the crank that would lower the mainsail, then gathered the sail into neat folds and lashed it down.

The boat leveled off.

But this was only a temporary measure. She needed time to think.

Well, first things first. She had to secure the boat. The easiest way would be to lower both sails and let the boat simply drift. But a boat adrift was helpless and could easily capsize. There was no way she could right a capsized boat. And then there was Aaron. Rachel hoped he was just unconscious. He might come to soon, and everything would be all right. If not, she would have to rope him down in case the boat tipped over.

OK. No problem, she thought. *I've done this a million times before. I could even do it in my sleep.* Then, despairingly, she realized that even in her dreams she could see what she was doing. A wave of helplessness washed over her.

She shook Aaron. "Wake up!" Tears raked her cheeks. "I want to go home! Take me home!" She pummeled his arms and chest. "It's all your fault!" she shouted at him. She collapsed onto the deck and wept uncontrollably.

Again the boat pitched and rolled. Rachel crawled to the skipper's seat behind the tiller. Strands of hair plastered her face, and her nose was running. *It's a good thing I can't see myself,* she said to herself. *I must look awful.*

Suddenly the sheer stupidity of this thought caused her to break into peals of laughter. It was as if the tight coil that had been her insides had suddenly sprung open. She was crying again, but with tears of laughter. She took a deep breath and wiped her nose on her sleeve.

"Folks," she announced into the wind. "This is your captain speaking! It looks like some rough weather up ahead, so better fasten those safety belts."

Rachel trimmed the sail for a close reach, which put her mainsail at a fairly generous angle to the wind. But her movements were awkward. She felt like an infant taking its first tentative steps.

Still, she managed to lash the rudder to turn the boat windward.

"OK! That's more like it." Next she turned the jib sail flat to the wind. The object was to have the two sails working against each other. The mainsail strained to push the boat in one direction, while the jib pulled it in another.

"Yes! Yahoo!" As the boat stalled in lightly rocking waters, Rachel gave a victory whoop and pumped her fist in the air.

With any luck, the squall would blow itself out or turn in another direction. Rachel crossed her fingers.

Next she scooped some salt water into a tin cup and tried to clean Aaron's wound. She laid him out flat, out of the sun.

She whipped off her belt and slipped the tongue under and out through the wooden deck slats, passing it over Aaron's waist, under a sleeve of his life jacket, and then under the slats on the other side. Rachel was worried about cinching it too tight, but she had to be sure to secure Aaron in case of a capsize.

When she finished she realized she was very thirsty. She crawled gingerly across the deck in search of the ditty bag. She found it and removed a plastic water bottle with a squeeze tube top. She angled the tube so that a dribble of water fell onto Aaron's lips. Next she took a long drink herself.

She then clipped the bottle onto a pin on her vest.

The sun was angled lower in the sky, and a cool steady breeze buffeted the boat. Even so, Rachel was drenched in sweat. The important thing was not to panic.

Fortunately the squall seemed to have blown itself out. A drizzle fell but then lightened, and Rachel could feel the sun warming her face. But that meant that before too long the sun would be going down. Rachel did not relish the idea of being adrift at night in a day sailor.

Another problem—a major problem—was that she couldn't be sure exactly where she was. Aaron probably would have maintained a course that hugged the shore. But after the accidental jibe, the boat could have been turned around. And because winds are notoriously unpredictable, she had no idea if the wind blowing now were true or not. One direction might take her on an open course out to sea. Another might ground her toward shore.

What she needed was a bearing of some kind. With the boat's running lights on, she could flip on her emergency strobe and hope that a commercial or sport fisherman headed for shore would spot her. It might work.

The pain in her shoulder had slackened somewhat. Even so, she felt a numbing fatigue. And a chilling mist was breaking over the bow. Rachel shivered and huddled lower against the helm. Her knees were cramping. The sail fluttered like empty bellows. Every few minutes she poured water over Aaron's forehead.

A decision had to be made.

"C'mon, Rachel," she scolded herself. "You know what to do. Just think. Visualize."

Visualize.

"Of course!" she shouted. She had made this run millions of times before. There wasn't a feature of the terrain she didn't know by heart. All she had to do was concentrate, to listen for something that might reveal her location. It could be anything. The faraway rumble of car traffic on the highway. Or a boat engine. Or a horn of some kind.

Even the sound of the wind might surrender some clue if only she listened hard enough.

She pressed her eyes tight and frowned with the effort. *C'mon.* The boat rocked gently, and she was distracted by the slapping of the halyards on the mast. Even the lulling sounds of waves bumping up against the hull and water splashing over the bow disturbed her concentration.

C'mon! C'mon! she thought impatiently. But no matter how hard she tried, she could not keep the noises of the boat from her thoughts. Her stomach did a flip-flop.

I'm not going to make it . . .

It was a voice that came bubbling up from somewhere deep inside her. The fear she had suppressed was returning. But now it was a hand with long fingers slashing at her insides, dragging her down.

"No!" she shouted. "I'm not going to give up! I'm not going to die!"

Suddenly the breeze that had rocked the boat stilled, and for a brief envelope in time it was so quiet that Rachel could hear her heart beating against her chest.

No, not her heart beating. A bell!

Rachel sat up straight and listened. A smile broke out over her face.

The bell buoy!

Instantly Rachel fell into action. She was a whirring machine, all memory and instinct. She imagined a straight line between her bow and the buoy and trimmed the sails to tack along a windward course, zigzagging the boat along that line. She mentally timed the bells. She could not afford to miss a single one and stray too far off course.

Each time the bell dinged she corrected her course to make certain the boat was trimmed in line with the buoy.

Rachel was too conscious of keeping the boat properly trimmed to take notice of the pattering of raindrops on the water. But quickly the pattering swelled into a loud drumming.

"No! The bell. I can't hear the bell!" Rachel shouted into the downpour. The skies ripped open, and the rain beat down like hammers on a tin ceiling.

Rachel screamed at the sky, "You can't do this! It's not fair. Not after all I've been through! Not now."

The rain washed down and then began to blow sideways.

Rachel began to smile.

"Yes! That's right! Head in to shore! That's it!" She sat up at the tiller and turned her ear toward open water.

And again she heard the bell buoy. Dead ahead. She felt suddenly calm and very alive.

Rachel could sense the skies clearing above her. The wind calmed and turned steady and true. She became conscious of her hand on the tiller and marveled at its sensitivity. Suddenly it was as if every sensation she had forbidden herself had returned. She was overwhelmed by the intensity and variety and fragrance of everything she touched and smelled. It was glorious!

The boat slipped easily through the water.

The bell was her heartbeat now. It was keeping her alive. She put the boat into a repeating circle that would sweep wide of the buoy—as if the boat were on a tether that swung around it.

Rachel flipped on the running lights and the hazard lights. They blinked continuously. A boat running in a circle is a universal distress signal. It was only a matter of time before some craft or rescue plane spotted her.

She had confronted her fear. She wasn't sure she had conquered it. She doubted she ever would. But she had found a way to manage it. There would be bad times ahead, she knew. And that was OK.

Rachel was cold and damp and hungry. But for the first time in a long time she was happy.

A moment later she heard Aaron groaning. She breathed a sigh of relief. Aaron lifted up his head, took one look at Rachel and grinned. He was rubbing the back of his head. "It didn't go exactly as I planned," he mumbled.

Rachel smiled back. "We're going to be OK."

She didn't see it, but a patrol cruiser was already heading in their direction.

THE DREAM OF AMY KNIGHT

"Are you sure?" she cried out happily. She gazed doubtfully into the boat.

Her husband turned to her and smiled. "Aye, I'm sure. You and the baby will have a grand time. It will be like floating on a cloud."

The sky was a beautiful bright blue. Not a cloud in sight. The sea tossed gently. The young husband helped his wife and baby into the boat.

"Just make yourself comfortable. Leave the rest to me." He slipped the watch from his trouser pocket, glanced at it, and smiled. "All ready, then?"

The woman grinned and nodded. Then she brought the baby up in her cradled arms and kissed the child on the cheek.

They were so happy.

In the distance, the dark clouds were gathering.

HER HEART WAS POUNDING in her chest.

"You don't understand. I saw her!"

"It was a nightmare, Amy. I know it seemed real. But that's what a nightmare is, honey."

Amy was in bed with the quilt pulled up under her folded arms. She glared at her mother, who was sitting on the edge of her bed. Amy listened angrily to the rain that slashed against her bedroom window.

She said simply, "I saw her. It wasn't a dream." Amy narrowed her eyes. "You don't believe me."

"Of course I believe you, Amy."

Amy slapped the quilt with her fists. "Then why are you treating me like a child?"

"Because you *are* a child, Amy. You remember what the doctors said? Amy?" Amy frowned and turned to look out the window.

Amy's mom smoothed back a damp tangle of hair from her daughter's forehead. "It's all right, darling. Go back to sleep." She turned to the window. "It's stopped raining. Everything will be alright now."

"How do you know?"

"Trust me." She patted Amy's hand reassuringly. "Sleep tight."

In her dark room Amy breathed the musty smell of sea water and rain that always followed a storm. The latch dropped on the bedroom door down the hall. Next came the sighing of bed springs as her mother climbed into bed, and muffled nighttime voices. Amy waited until the voices died away. Then she threw off the covers and stood at her bedroom window. A gust of wind on the ocean stirred the silvered moonlight like sparkling autumn leaves.

Clusters of stars blinked in the night sky.

Amy stood for a long time without breathing. Then she whispered, "I know you're out there."

The next day Amy came down to breakfast earlier than usual and informed her parents that she would be bicycling to the library and would probably not be back for lunch. She acted as if nothing had happened.

"It's raining again," her father informed her. "Don't forget to take your raincoat and galoshes."

Amy munched on a piece of toast. "Sure, dad."

"Drink your—" Her father frowned as the door slapped shut.

Amy rode her bike down a long road. One side was crowded with tiny summer cottages. On the other side was the sea. Raindrops stung her eyes. The center of town was at the end of the road. Amy turned up Mercer Street to the Town Square. The library was the big brick building that fronted the square. She padlocked her bike outside the library, climbed up the wooden steps, and walked inside. The librarian, Mr. Terwilliger, greeted her warmly.

"Ah, Amy! My favorite customer."

"Hey, Mr. Terwilliger!" She shook herself dry. Rainwater splattered everywhere.

"Please, Amy!" he protested. "I've already taken one bath this morning. It's too early for another."

Amy grinned. She knew he wasn't really cross.

Mr. Terwilliger was only a bit taller than Amy. He always wore the same baggy suit and oval, wireframed glasses. His face was as fat and round as the moon, and his thick bristly hair reminded Amy of steel wool.

He loved books almost as much as Amy did.

"What can I do for you today? Did you know we're having a special sale? All the Lois Lowry you can read. Absolutely free. Or perhaps your tastes run more to the classics? A little Dickens, perhaps?"

"Sounds great, Mr. Terwilliger. But—" Amy reached out and put a hand on his shoulder. "I have something serious to discuss with you. You had better sit down, Mr. Terwilliger."

The old man pursed his lips. He peered at Amy over his glasses. "This does sound serious, Amy."

"Quite serious."

"Serious talk calls for cocoa. You wait here. I'll be right back."

He came back a short time later with two steaming cups of cocoa.

All of a sudden there was a deafening clap of thunder. The giant library windows shuddered and shook, and the sky collapsed in a gust of rain that pummeled the roof like a flurry of fists.

"Gosh," said Mr. Terwilliger as he settled into his favorite chair. "That was a doozy."

Amy sat down in a chair opposite the librarian. Her cocoa was cradled between her knees. "I'd better start at the beginning."

Amy told him about her dream.

"It's like I'm *in* the dream, but *not* in it. Both at the same time. D'ya know what I mean?"

He nodded politely, not quite understanding.

"I think I'm drowning. At least, that's what it feels like. I can feel hands grabbing at me. But they never catch hold of me. My hair is floating around my face and I try to scream, but no words come out. I hear someone calling my name. But it's coming from far away. Then I wake up."

The old librarian nodded and furrowed his brow.

"That's when I see her," Amy continued.

"Who, Amy?"

"The woman from my dream. She is standing at the end of the jetty in front of our cottage. She just stands there and stares out at the sea."

Mr. Terwilliger leaned forward. "You mean, the same woman from your dream?"

"Yeah," said Amy. "Then you believe me?"

"Of course I believe you."

"My parents think I'm making it up," snorted Amy. "They don't believe a word I say." She looked down at her sneakers, embarrassed. "Neither do all the doctors. They say the nightmares are symptoms of" —she made quotation marks with her fingers—"'an *overactive imagination.*' I mean, how stupid is that?"

She sighed wearily. "Nobody believes me."

Mr. Terwilliger steepled his hands. "Can you remember anything else?"

Amy stared off into the distance, then said, "Yeah. I think the woman's crying, or it might just be the rain on her face. But she looks very sad."

"You are certain you saw this . . . *ghost*?"

Amy nodded

Mr. Terwilliger sighed. "What we need is proof."

After dinner that night Amy watched a boring movie on television. Then she went to bed. She was drifting off when her father came into the bedroom.

"Feeling OK?" he asked.

Amy smiled and turned to face him. "Yeah, dad. Just a little tired."

Her father leaned over and kissed Amy softly on the forehead.

"Sweet dreams, Amy."

She woke in the middle of the night, the dream still fresh in her mind. Hurrying over to the window, Amy saw the lonely woman standing at the end of the stone jetty. This time Amy was prepared. She threw on her jacket and crept downstairs. The moon was out and the grass silvered with light. Amy tiptoed toward the jetty.

The woman looked as if she were made up entirely of flowing white veils. She was staring out to sea. Amy felt a chill run down her spine as she scrambled over the rocks to where the mysterious woman stood.

"It's me," Amy said. She was close enough to touch her.

The woman wheeled around. Her turning felt to Amy like a sudden blast of wind. An astonished look was on her face. Amy instinctively reached out a hand. The woman herself reached out. For a brief moment their fingers became entwined, and something was pressed into Amy's palm.

Suddenly Amy lost her footing and stumbled backward into the sea. The water was so cold it numbed her skin. She couldn't remember how long she'd been screaming before her father flew out the back door and saw her struggling in the dark water. Then she blacked out.

The doctor came and examined her in her room. Afterward Amy heard him talking with her parents.

A short time later her mother entered the room.

"What happened, Amy?"

Amy shook her head. "Just a bad dream."

Her mother kissed her good-night. Amy waited for her mother to leave before reaching under her mattress. The watch the woman had slipped into her hand felt cold.

The next afternoon Amy bicycled to the library and found Mr. Terwilliger reshelving a cart of books.

"What is it, Amy?"

Amy smiled. "Proof."

The librarian looked confused. "Proof? What kind of proof?"

Amy showed him the watch.

Mr. Terwilliger gasped. "Where did you get this?"

"*She* gave it to me."

His eyes became round as saucers. "Holy smokes. Would you look at that." Mr. Terwilliger stood up hastily. "Amy, there is someone I have to see right away. Will you be OK here by yourself?"

Amy nodded and resumed reading her book.

The afternoon drifted on.

The giant clock on the wall tick-tocked away as the sky turned from angry black to dismal gray, then to black again. Nearby the sea had turned gray, too. A dingy wet gray that reminded Amy of soggy old newspapers.

After a while Amy grew tired of reading. It was getting late, and Mr. Terwilliger had still not returned. She decided to leave. She would talk again with the librarian tomorrow. That night the dream was more vivid than ever before.

The woman clutched at the side of the boat.

"What is it? What's the matter, Ian?" Her scarf danced in the wind. The smooth sea had turned rough. Whitecaps flecked the dark blue water. The wooden boat was tossing about.

Her husband reassured her. "It's nothing. Just a bit of a kickup. There's nothing to fear."

The baby began to cry.

The woman hummed a lullaby. The little boat rocked like a cradle on the wide open sea.

THE NEXT DAY Amy found Mr. Terwilliger sitting in his favorite chair, drinking tea and brooding. The gold pocket watch sat on the table beside him.

"Tell me again where you got it," he said to Amy.

She sighed wearily. "I told you already. *She* gave it to me."

He hefted the watch in his palm. "I took the liberty of having this watch appraised by an old friend of mine who collects antiques. It is very old. I expect you knew that already."

Amy nodded. "Is it worth much?"

Mr. Terwilliger pushed up his eyebrows. Behind his glasses his blue eyes twinkled. "Actually, yes. It is. *Quite* a lot in fact. Amy, this watch is solid gold."

Amy sat back in her chair and whistled.

"Exactly. But that's not all. I want to show you something." Mr. Terwilliger pried open the watch. Inside the cover was an old photo of a husband and wife and a little girl. Amy felt a chill run down her spine. The little girl was younger than Amy.

But they looked like twins.

"I couldn't believe it myself when I saw it. The resemblance is uncanny."

"Who is she?" asked Amy.

He shook his head. "I'm not sure. It could be anybody. This area has always been very popular with tourists. But there is one thing I do know. Amy, this watch is over one hundred years old!"

He looked hard at Amy.

Mr. Terwilliger leaned forward and handed Amy the photograph. "I want you to study the picture very hard. Does anyone else in it look familiar?"

Amy frowned. "But it's a hundred years old?"

"Just try."

Amy studied the photograph. The woman was young and very pretty. Her long dark hair was pulled up into a heavy bundle at her neck. She wore a white dress with a high collar. Her eyes were a deep and dark brown.

Amy gasped. "She's the woman in my dream."

Mr. Terwilliger nodded his head slowly. "I was afraid of that."

The boat rocked unsteadily as the wind bullied the tiny craft. Clouds, dark and ominous, blotted out the blue sky. The shoreline, only moments before so close she felt she could reach out and touch it, was shrinking away to nothingness. All around her the sea grumbled, cold and dark and forbidding. The wind shrieked. The woman clutched the infant desperately and looked worriedly at her husband. He was hunched over the tiller, his hair whipping in the wind. Suddenly the boat climbed as a giant swell bellied beneath it and the young woman screamed into the jaws of a howling wind.

"Hold onto the baby!" The wind shredded his words like paper.

"Take this!" He handed her the gold watch, "It's all I have left. It's worth a lot."

"No! We'll be all right. You promised!"

The boat lurched suddenly, the bottom of the world dropped away, and the sceaming woman fell swiftly through space.

HER DAUGHTER'S SCREAMS awakened Sheila Knight.

She ran blindly down the hall and flung open the door. Amy lay in bed. She was thrashing about. Moonlight dappled the quilt, which lay all twisted on the bed. Sweat drenched Amy's face, and tears raked her cheeks.

"Amy!" her mom cried out, grabbing her daughter's wrists. She leaned down to kiss the girl's fevered forehead. She tasted something strange. Suddenly her skin went cold as ice.

Salt water.

"Amy!"

MR. TERWILLIGER SET aside the broom and dustpan and lowered himself into the old leather recliner. A steaming mug of tea brooded on a side table. The library would not open officially for another hour, but the old librarian savored his quiet time.

He couldn't stop thinking about Amy. It might have been a coincidence. She might have found the watch in her wanderings. She could have dug it up along the shore in front of her family's cottage. Did she make up the story about the woman on the beach? Kids are always making up stories. And Amy had one of the most vivid imaginations he had come across.

But she seemed *so sure*.

And what about his friend the antique dealer, who had marveled at how well preserved the watch was?

He had to find out who the family was in the photograph. It was a long shot, but maybe the answer had been under his nose all the time. He pulled out a set of old keys on a giant loop and walked to the back of the library. The door that led to the archives was hard to open. Someone had painted it shut. He had to lower his shoulder against the door before it gave way.

Old newspapers were collected in huge black binders with pebbly covers. The pages were yellow and very dusty. Every time he turned a page he sneezed. He checked his watch: It was a little after ten o'clock.

By noon he had poured over a dozen binders with no luck. He decided to try just one more. A headline caught his attention.

"Aha!" he brightened. He read the article excitedly, then glanced around the room apprehensively. "I could lose my job for this," he grumbled as he ripped out the page.

"I'M SORRY TO be calling so late, but I was wondering if I might speak with Amy for a minute?"

"Amy's in bed," said her father. "It's after ten o'clock."

"Oh dear. It is rather urgent that I speak with her."

"Is there a problem?" asked Amy's father.

"Yes, actually. Rather a big problem. A matter of life and death."

"Who is this? What's going on?

"I'll be right over."

FRANK KNIGHT JUMPED angrily to his feet. "Let me get this straight. What you're saying is, my daughter has seen a ghost. A real ghost. And you think this ghost is going to *kidnap* Amy."

In a chair in the front room of the rented cottage the old librarian drank a cup of tea. "That is correct. The woman is grief stricken over the death of her child. She simply wants her Amy back."

Amy's mother and father looked at one another, stunned.

Mr. Terwilliger said, "Look. I know this sounds strange. But consider the facts. Your name is Knight. So was theirs. This is the house they lived in. And what Amy says she saw in her dreams fits exactly the description of what happened." He removed the faded newspaper clipping from his shirt pocket and read: "Two members of a family summering on Massapequa were drowned when their sailboat capsized in rough seas after the weather turned squalid. The husband, Silas Knight, and his infant daughter both died. The wife, Sara Knight, survived. Silas Knight was believed to be an inexperienced sailor."

Frank Knight sighed. "All this is just coincidence." He turned again to his wife. "You don't believe any of this, do you?"

She was silent.

Frank Knight cupped his hands to his head and sank into the couch. "I can't believe this."

Mr. Terwilliger then related local rumors. "When the husband and baby died, the townsfolk around here were sympathetic. But it wasn't long before gossip started about how the husband and baby drowned but the wife survived. It was said that she . . . abandoned her baby . . . to save herself."

"That's horrible!" exclaimed Sheila Knight.

"Yes. Anyway, there wasn't much the widow could do but keep to herself. People started calling her 'The Baby Killer of Massapequa.' Folks shunned her. Cursed her name so she should never have a moment's peace. Practically everyone in the town believed in the curse ever since."

"What happened to her?" asked Sheila Knight.

"As far as I know, she died friendless and alone. Though folks say she still haunts the shore at night, waiting for her husband and baby to return. But maybe it isn't the curse that torments her, but the grief of her own heart."

Frank Knight sat down heavily. "It's just a stupid old rumor," he muttered. "Besides, you said it all happened a hundred years ago."

"Correction," Mr. Terwilliger amended. "A hundred years ago . . . *tonight*."

Sheila Knight, her shoulders slumped, uttered a helpless groan. She turned to Mr. Terwilliger. "The child's name. The one who drowned."

Mr. Terwilliger nodded.

"Her name was Amy."

Bundles of darkened clouds appeared to merge with the sea in one raging maelstrom. The boat pitched sideways, flinging the woman overboard. "Silas!" she screamed. "I can't swim!"

She was sinking. "Dear God!" she screamed, tears stinging her eyes. "Take me, but save the child!" A rogue wave washed over her, and she gulped sea water. Coughing and spitting, she hurriedly unwrapped the sodden scarf from around her neck and tried to lash her infant daughter to the boat. Suddenly she and the boat scaled the face of a great black wave. The child screamed. Her mother tried to reach her, to strengthen the knot. "Please hold on, Amy. Please hold on!" Suddenly the boat rocked, and the baby was thrown into the dark water.

"Noooooo!" wailed Amy. She jerked up in bed and ran to the window. The rain was rippling down in great waves, but at the end of the point she could see the woman silhouetted against the sky. Amy flew down the stairs, threw open the door, and raced headlong across the dunes.

Suddenly the woman turned, and Amy could see her face. Her hair was limp and tangled, and her eyes were deep dark hollows that were dead to the world. Amy crawled up a jumble of rocks, moving closer.

The figure pulled back.

"Wait!" Amy screamed. She pulled the watch from her pocket and held it out to the woman by its chain.

The woman reached out a hand. Her fingers were like wisps of smoke that curled around the watch, then twisted around Amy's wrist.

Amy dug in her heels. Something was wrong. "No. It wasn't your fault!" she pleaded. "I know what happened. It wasn't your fault."

Amy. My darling.

"No! I'm not Amy!"

My darling child. Come to me.

Icy fingers climbed up her arm. Another hand reached for her. Amy tried to swat it away.

"Amy!" Her father was running toward her from the house.

"Daddy! Help!"

Her father raced across the beach and scrambled over the rocks. The woman raised a hand to ward him off. Amy tugged and tried to break free. "Daddy!" She could feel ice running like blood through her veins. Already her left arm was as white as a sheet.

Amy had an idea. *The watch!* She snatched it from the ghost's hand and hid it behind her back. The ghost let out a terrifying cry. She loosened her grip on Amy and lunged for the watch.

Noooooooooooo!

But it was too late. The ghost wailed as Amy threw the watch with all her might. It sailed out in a long arc over the sea and dropped out of sight forever. Amy turned.

The ghost had vanished.

Her father wrapped his arms around her and led her back to the house. Amy turned around for one last look, but the ghost was nowhere in sight. She took her father's hand, and they both walked silently back to the cottage.

PREDATOR

THE SMELL OF blood aroused his keen senses. As he approached the much smaller fish, he noticed the animal had been partially devoured. *Nice work,* thought the shark.

He began to circle the half-eaten tuna, slowly, cautiously. You could never be sure of anything. Not these days, anyway. The shark had traveled hundreds of miles in search of food. He had not eaten in many days. The oil in his liver had sustained him and freed him from the need to kill. But the hunger had returned.

Propelling himself upward with a slight flick of his powerful tail, he glided up to the tuna for a closer inspection. The animal had been hacked in half. Ribbons of entrails dangled from the corpse.

Hunger gnawed at him.

The water around the tuna swelled with rich tasting blood and precious fatty oils. Yet the shark hesitated. Something about the shape of the bite struck him as odd. The predators he knew left a curve-shaped bite. This was straight.

Humans.

He'd come across these predators a few times. They hunted mostly from structures above the water. And they used giant curved bones to pull animals from the sea.

The shark shivered with disgust.

Often the animal pulled from the water would be horribly mutilated and then dumped back into the sea. What was the purpose? Guts and entrails and huge chunks of delicious meat discarded and left to rot? It made no sense to the shark.

They were not true hunters.

The shark brooded as he circled the mutilated tuna.

He remembered once biting into a lovely chunk of mackerel. Then a stabbing pain crippled him. A sharp curve of spiked bone impaled itself inside the flesh of his lower jaw. He was hauled upward on the hook. His flesh tore and ripped. The pain turned him into a thrashing demon.

He writhed and slashed at the hook and finally was able to free himself.

The agony he experienced that day he would remember forever. He had learned his lesson. These human hunters from above the sea were not to be trifled with.

Unhappily for the shark, humans returned daily to hunt the ocean. And with each return their numbers increased. Already the shark had been forced to abandon favored for less-familiar waters farther south. Waters that once abounded with seal or stingray were disappearing. Prey was harder to find.

He eyed the mutilated tuna one last time and swam off.

The shark kept moving. He had no choice. The more scarce the prey, the farther the shark needed to swim for his next meal. And the period between meals kept lengthening. Where would it end? Was it this strange human predator who was taking away his food?

Once he had encountered a human, just about snout to snout. The human had entered the water inside a skeleton made up of hard spines. The human had a thick smelly skin that lacked scales. Enormous eyes covered its face, and a hole in its face leaked bubbles continuously. The shark simply ignored the ungainly and unappetizing creature.

But it seemed to beckon to the shark.

What was on its mind? What did it want?

Perhaps it was sick and had been rejected by the group? Or perhaps it was some kind of peace offering?

If it was an offering, it was an *awfully puny* one.

More out of curiosity than anything the shark swam past the skeleton cage, then gave it a quick flip with his tail. The shark remembered fondly the astonished expression on the human's face. Its eyes grew as round as clams.

Just for fun the shark bumped the cage again, a little harder. Much to his surprise, the spines snapped easily. This alarmed the creature inside the cage. It thrashed about wildly. It emitted a frenzied burst of bubbles. It cowered and kicked and flapped its fins.

Well, the shark thought, no fish willingly becomes a shark's meal. He couldn't really blame it. But the truth was, the shark had already lost interest in the human as a menu item.

He needed meat rich in fat. That was what sustained him. Seal was ideal.

But the seals had been driven off. By those humans. They hunted the seals with their spears and their hooks and their clubs. They overhunted the mackerel too. And the sea turtle.

Hunger was overwhelming the shark.

He had no choice but to leave the relative safety of deep water for the shallow waters toward shore. It was a huge risk. Humans had the advantage of numbers closer to shore. But the shark amused himself with this thought: *Perhaps I shall tip the balance. Then they will know how it feels.*

To the shark, it seemed only fair.

The shark avoided humans whenever possible. As food they were loathsome. He only attacked when forced to.

But humans attacked relentlessly.

He had seen his own kind slaughtered many times. They were harvested for their fins. A hunter would hook a shark, slice off the fin, and dump the live animal overboard. The wounded shark was helpless, of course. Its fate was always the same: It bled to death, slowly and agonizingly.

The shark killed once every four or five days. And always he sought out the already dying, the sick or the old. But humans killed many hundreds of times a day. And always they sought out the largest and finest.

It made no sense.

The shark swam on with flagging hope. The hunger pains were unbearable. He was exhausted. His muscles ached.

"I must eat something. And soon."

It did not matter what. He came upon a section of the sea that rose up along a steep incline. A net had been dropped along a line that stretched many miles in either direction. He could see very little through the net, but he could smell a school of some kind of fish on the other side. His senses electrified.

He passed along the net. It was very strong, and he could not push through it.

He butted along the net, searching for an opening. *Let me through!*

He could smell them now. A large school of fish, hundreds perhaps, splashed away happily on the other side. His brain boiled with a kind of hunger fever. Nothing mattered but to feed.

He circled and lunged and caught the net low along the seabed in his jaw and whipped his head back and forth. Again and again he struck, each time catching the same section of net, his serrated teeth gnashing and grinding it. He was exhausted. Just one more pass.

The shark circled and swam away, then turned back and lunged.

The net peeled away, and the shark slipped under and through silently.

His senses bristled. Humans were gathered close to shore. The shark could not believe his luck. There must have been hundreds of them! They were kicking and screaming and splashing about happily at the surface, oblivious to his slow approach.

It would last less than a minute at most. Then the water would clear, and he would return to the deep.

He had no choice.

He was the great white shark, *Carcharodon carcharias*.

But that day he would be known as the white death.

You'll Be Sorry

HIS MOTHER CALLED down to him: "*Do* try and behave yourself, Harold. Just this once." Harold looked up from the beach and glowered. His mother was lounging on the deck of their second-floor hotel room, sipping a glass of orange juice. "Like I have a choice," he grumbled.

"What's that, darling?"

"Nothing," snarled Harold.

She put down her drink and posed for him. "What do you think, Harold?"

When his father surprised the family by announcing that they would be vacationing in Florida for Christmas, Harold's mother ran right out to buy new bathing suits. Harold had been appalled. "I'm not wearing *this*," he shrieked. It was a pair of bathing trucks with a matching shirt, decorated with cartoon seashells that spelled out FUN IN THE SUN!

"Don't I look smart?" she chirped. "I feel just like a famous Hollywood movie star!" Her arms and legs were as long and thin as broomsticks. Her skin was so pale it glowed. Her head was swathed in a scarf, and her jet black sunglasses were as big as hubcaps.

To Harold, she looked like a giant bug. "This vacation stinks."

"Don't be such an old poop."

He shoved his pudgy fists into his shorts pockets. His cheeks puffed angrily and he felt like kicking something. Really hard. But all there was around was sand. And ocean. The ocean stretched for miles like a giant mirror to the sky. But nothing he saw appealed to Harold. All he could think about was his cluttered bedroom back home and his top-secret experiments.

Harold had turned his bedroom into a laboratory for dissecting things. Frogs, mostly. And lizards he caught in the woods or under barrels and rocks. Harold wasn't interested in science. He just liked to be mean. He kept the dissected parts in empty jam jars and hid them under his bed and in his closet.

Just then a sand fly bumbled onto his leg. "Ahhh," Harold whispered delightedly. His frown collapsed into a nasty grin. The fly was huge so it was certain to make a huge SPLAT. Harold hoisted his arm like a guillotine blade. Then, his grin flaring, he brought his hand down with a resounding SMACK.

His mother—startled—jumped. "Jeez, Harold!" she cried. Her sunglasses tilted clumsily. "I nearly had a heart attack."

Harold grinned triumphantly, "I told you so." He neatly scraped the dead fly from his leg with the tip of his finger and brought it up close. "Wow!" he said, impressed. It *was* huge. He said in his fake announcer voice: "Last call for Flight 100 nonstop to Deadville. Have a nice trip!" He curled back the finger under the tip of his thumb, like a catapult, and flicked.

"You shouldn't kill things."

Harold glared at his little sister. He'd practically forgotten she was there. Maggie was wearing a purple Barney bathing suit and plastic Goofy sunglasses. He glared at her and sat back in his beach chair.

"Why are you so mean?" she asked in a tiny voice.

"Listen, snotbreath. I told you to keep your trap shut."

"You'll be sorry."

"Oh, yeah? How'd you like me to make you eat sand?"

"Mommmmy!!!!"

Harold snickered as his little sister ran whimpering across the beach and up the steps of the hotel. But his gloating didn't last long. Bored, he decided to take a walk along the shore. Maybe he could dig up something to dissect.

Harold brightened when he spied a flock of seagulls idling at the water's edge. He rummaged in the sand for a rock. He flung the rock as hard as he could.

"Hah!" he shouted when his missile plonked a birds tail followed by an explosion of flapping and terrified squawking. The conked bird careened drunkenly, then flew away over the sea.

"You'll be sorry!" someone shouted. Harold spun round, but there was nobody anywhere near.

Suddenly his attention was drawn to a commotion down the beach. A group of sunbathers had splashed into the surf and stood huddled in a circle. Harold ran over. "What's going on?" A woman with a big hat was shaking her head and covering her mouth with her hand. Harold thought she might start bawling any minute. She pointed down at the sand. "A whale has beached itself."

"Let me through!" Harold barked. He sloshed through the water and pushed his way past a forest of legs. He had never seen anything so big. It was rolled over on its side, and a huge shiny black eye stared up at him. Its jaw lay open, and Harold could see its thick lolling tongue.

"Is it dead?" asked Harold excitedly.

"No," answered a man in floppy swimming trucks. He was wearing a baseball cap with a huge bill. He added solemnly, "Not yet."

The whale made a rude wheezing sound. "I bet a hunter harpooned it!" Harold searched along the sleek flanks for a bloody hole. "Cripes," he said, disappointed.

People in the crowd were talking in low whispers. The man in the cap dipped a plastic beach bucket into the surf, then splashed the water over the whale. He did this several times.

"What're you doing?" asked Harold.

"Trying to keep it cool. The poor thing probably got confused and beached itself in the low tide. If we don't keep it wet, it'll die of suffocation."

Harold glowed excitedly. "Really?"

"What else should we do?" asked a man urgently.

I know what I'd do, Harold mused.

That night at dinner, Harold was inconsolable. Not only had the whale not died, but a rescue team from a local university had arrived in a special ambulance with a huge crane to lift the whale out of the surf and race it back to a customized tank where it could be nursed back to health.

"This vacation stinks," Harold grumbled.

His little sister sniffed, then said "phew!"

"Now that you mention it," his mother added, "you do smell a bit *ripe*, Harold."

Harold sniffed under both armpits. "You're nuts."

"No," his father said. "She's right, Harold. You smell like a dead fish. Oh! That reminds me." His father announced that he had chartered a boat for a private fishing trip the very next morning.

"Fishing?" Harold pushed out his lip, skeptical. It sounded like something that would involve a lot of work and not much fun. "I thought this was supposed to be a vacation."

"It is, Harold," his father assured him. Behind his smiling lips, his big teeth shined whitely. "You'll have a good time. I promise."

The boat was named *Sal 'T' Scupper.*

"On account of my name is Sal!" bellowed the captain of the boat as he helped them aboard. "Get it?" After they settled in, the boat roared to life and chugged out of the harbor into the open sea. Captain Sal promised that he was taking them to a place tourists never went.

That was more than two hours ago. "Where is this place?" moaned Harold dismally. "Cleveland?"

"Won't be much farther!" yelled Captain Sal.

79

It was very hot on the boat, and Harold thought he was going to be sick. The sun hammered down on his head and shoulders and glared off the water. The boat tipped lazily from side to side. Occasionally, shallow waves would hummock under the boat and lift it unsteadily, and a foul taste would elevator up from Harold's stomach to his throat. A smelly vapor billowed out his cheeks. A pungent odor, like dead fish.

"Big brother doesn't look so good," his sister giggled.

His mother was tittering as well. Harold turned lumpily from the rail. Maggie beamed at him with childish innocence. Harold glared at her venomously. "You'll get yours," he promised her darkly.

"Don't be such a baby, Harold," his father teased. Just then the chugging of the engines stopped. He clapped Harold on the shoulder. "What do you say we catch some fish, huh?"

Harold nodded, bent over, and vomited on his father's shoes.

The pill helped settle his stomach. But it made him drowsy. He decided to take a nap downstairs. It was a relief to be somewhere cool, away from the relentless glare of the hot sun. It was dark in the cabin, but he could hear his family walking around on deck. Harold lay down on a cot and fell asleep.

He dreamed he was inside a closed coffin. Only this coffin was at the bottom of the sea, because when he tried to breathe he choked on salt water. It was pitch black, and he clawed at the lid with his fingers until they were raw. He woke up screaming and banged his head on the cabin roof.

He rubbed his head, and after a while he felt better. At least his stomach wasn't doing flip-flops. He decided to climb up on deck and explore. At the back of the boat he walked over to what looked like a large cooler. He lifted open the lid and saw the cooler was filled with fish. The salt water smelled horrible, and clumps of fish guts and ropy strings of blood clogged the surface. "Neat," said Harold.

Harold looked around to make sure he was alone. His mother was lounging at the front of the boat, working on her tan, and Harold could hear his father and little sister laughing and giggling as they fished.

Rummaging under a seat cushion, Harold found a utility box filled with knives. One in particular caught his eye. It had a large flat blade with a ferocious-looking barbed notch at the shank. It practically winked at him and said, "Take me." Then he grabbed an especially large fish by the tail and heaved it out of the box. It flopped heavily to the deck. At first he thought it might be dead.

"No fair," he whined. Harold took the knife and poked. The fish came to life suddenly. It wriggled and writhed. Harold brought the needle-sharp point of the knife close to the bulbous glassy eye. The fish jerked, but Harold grabbed hold of it and gave the blade a sharp twist.

There was a sudden gasp.

Harold twisted around so fast that he nearly tipped himself over. "It wasn't me!" he said hastily, expecting to see his mother or father glowering down at him. He had tucked the knife up under his shirt. But no one was watching him. *Oh well*, thought Harold. Then he smiled. *Maybe Maggie stuck herself with a fishhook.*

He knelt down again and searched around the fish for the eye. Suddenly the fish lunged at Harold and bit him on the arm.

Harold stumbled to his feet in a blind panic and crashed backward. Dozens of fishing rods and grappling hooks and nets came clattering down on his head. Harold spied what looked like a machete. It had a blade as long as his arm. He grabbed it, swung it over his head, and brought it crashing down.

A fish head skidded and spun sideways from the blade. Harold was sweating with effort. His hands and shirtfront were smeared with blood and guts and silvery scales. He could hardly breathe.

From the pilothouse came the voice of Captain Sal. "There are less extreme methods for gutting a fish. If you're interested."

That night at dinner Harold's family acted strangely. It was as if they had suddenly been transformed into The World's Most Perfect Family. Even Maggie was on her best behavior. Harold had prepared himself for the worst. But it never happened. Nobody mentioned anything about him getting sick. Nothing was said of the undignified episode with the fish. They all chattered as if nothing at all unusual had happened. Harold was deeply suspicious. Then he discovered why.

When the waiter glided up to the table, the three of them disappeared behind their menus. "It all looks so good!" his mother said.

The waiter, pleased, obliged with a bow. "All of our specials are quite excellent, Madam."

His father looked up from his menu. "Tell me, what's your special soup tonight?"

The waiter smiled appreciatively. "Ah. A fragrant bouillabaisse. Most excellent." His father suddenly hiccuped, and Harold frowned. *Was his father laughing?* wondered Harold. He looked around. All three of them, it seemed to Harold, appeared to be on the verge of some hilarious punchline.

"Bouillabaisse," his mother repeated, as if intrigued. "What is that exactly?"

"Fish heads."

The laughter burst out like thunder.

Under his own dark cloud, Harold sat and smoldered. *Just wait*, he promised them silently, *you'll be sorry*.

That night as Harold was brushing his teeth he noticed a strange rash on his arm where the fish had bitten him. It was not painful or itchy, but the skin was rough and raised, like scar tissue.

Harold scratched it anyway. A quarter-sized flake of skin dropped off. He picked it up from the sink and examined it. It was hard and transparent. He picked again at his arm. The skin was ridged like scales.

That night he had another horrible dream. This time he was on a boat in a storm. A huge wave upset the boat, and Harold was flung overboard. The water was dark and cold, and he held his breath. It felt as if a huge weight were pressing down on his chest.

When he couldn't hold his breath anymore, he gasped. But instead of inhaling salt water, he could breathe. Harold felt relieved. It felt as if he were floating in a warm tub. It was actually quite pleasant. He tried swimming. It was as easy as running. He darted this way and that as easily as a fish. *Hey, this is fun!* he thought. That was when he discovered that his hands were no longer separate wiggling fingers but were joined by a fleshy web. His hands were covered completely in scales.

"I'm a fish!" he chortled.

He felt something nibbling at his toe, delicately. Harold giggled. "Stop it!" he said, wriggling about in the water. "You're tickling me." Then he felt a sharp pain on the back of his neck. "Ouch!" he shouted. From the depths of the dark water a huge fish rushed at him suddenly and lunged at his eyes, snapping hungrily with ragged, serrated teeth. Harold was terrified.

"Get away from me!" he shouted.

He tried to use his arms to bat away the fish, but there was nothing there to bat with. It was as if his arms were pinned to his sides with rope. The fish rushed at him again. He whipped his head back and around. "Leave me alone!" he wailed.

Suddenly his leg erupted in fire. Another fish bit down hard on his leg. The water around him was swarming with fish, all of them thrashing and snapping and slashing at him with razor-sharp teeth. Harold started crying.

In his dream he heard a voice: "I told you you'd be sorry."

Harold awoke in the hospital with a bulky patch plastered over his left eye. His head and arms felt numb, and he could not move his neck. A doctor was talking with his parents in a discouraged tone of voice. His mother began whimpering.

"What happened?" Harold wanted to ask. But the words wouldn't come. His mouth felt funny. His whole face felt rubbery. It reminded him of the time he got a shot of novocaine from the dentist. *What's going on? WHAT'S GOING ON?!*

"Well," his father said finally, "if you can't treat him, who can?"

The doctor shook his head, stumped. "Well," he said, "there's always Sea World."

The Most Beautiful Day of the Year

United States Coast Guard Station,
Taholah, Washington. 4:50 P.M.

WHEN THE DOOR flew open, Lieutenant Alger spun around in his chair and threw up his hands against the sudden blast of wind and water.

"Close the door!" The lieutenant had no idea his superior, Captain Anderson, was standing in the doorway. "Uh, sorry, sir . . . I—I thought you were Jeffries."

The smile on Captain Anderson's face eased the lieutenant's anxiety, and Alger breathed a sigh of relief. Anderson heaved the station door closed. He shook himself out of his cumbersome rain gear, motioned silently for Alger to return to his post, then joined him at the control console.

The lighthouse station had been blindsided by a storm that had seemingly appeared out of nowhere. Anderson could not recall a storm of such compressed magnitude and violence, yet radar had picked up nothing. One minute it was warm and sunny, the next . . .

Anderson placed a soggy bag of sandwiches on the table. "Better keep that pot of coffee going," he instructed Alger. "This looks to be a long night."

A sudden flurry of inky rain swept up the face of the lighthouse station and hurtled against the windows, buckling them. The wind moaned and howled, and for a moment it seemed to both men that the station might be uprooted. Light flashed like a heartbeat.

"I wonder how many more blows like that this old tower can take," Alger said nervously. Anderson had been wondering the same thing.

"Where's Jeffries?"

Alger glanced at the clock on the wall. It read 4:59. "Due any minute, sir"

"Good. We'll need every available hand. OK, let's have it, lieutenant."

Alger looked up from the radar screen and shook his head, baffled. "I just don't get it. No depression curves on the radar. Not a trace of anything. As far as our instruments are concerned, this storm doesn't exist. Now comes word of a Class 4 system touching down in northern Alaska. In late October? That's nuts. None of this makes any sense."

Anderson sat down next to Alger. "Whether any of this makes sense to you is not our concern, lieutenant. The fact is, this coast guard station currently finds itself smack-dab in the center of a gale force storm, with reports that a potential hurricane is roaring down the coast and could touch down directly on us. And we have no idea how many distressed craft may be out there right now. Am I right?"

Alger sighed, then nodded gravely.

"What's important now is trying to determine the hurricane's course. Hopefully it will take itself on a westward trajectory and head harmlessly out to sea. But—" The captain got up and crossed over the room to a map on the wall. He traced his fingers along a slanting line. "The danger is if she swings southward. What's her current speed?"

"Sixty-eight."

Anderson winced. She was gaining speed. He did some quick mental calculations. Based on its speed and approximate location, the hurricane would touch down on the Washington coast in approximately three hours. That was an eternity in the lifetime of a storm. Anything could happen. Meanwhile an open channel hurricane warning had been issued for the area. The Alaska Coast Guard would have already broadcast its own advisories.

Anderson relaxed a bit. He stepped to the window. It was like staring into the mouth of a deep dark tunnel. He couldn't imagine the terror of a fisherman caught in the broadside of a storm. It wasn't just the horror of drowning. That was bad enough. It was the aching loneliness of being lost at sea, alone.

The lighthouse was pounded by another bullying gust of wind. Pellets of rain battered it. Anderson smiled ruefully, recalling a saying that a sailor should never set sail with a guilty conscience. For the sea has a long memory and will exact her own justice, by and by.

An anxious Alger interrupted his thoughts: "Mayday alert, sir!"

Anderson turned just as a burst of sound came crackling from the shortwave radio. Anderson strained to hear, but the voice drifted in and out.

"Can you identify?"

Alger shook his head. "Negative. The signal keeps breaking up. It—" Alger frowned with concentration. "Hold on. I think it's coming in."

Suddenly another burst came from the shortwave.

"Mayday! Mayday! Can you hear me? Mayday! This is the Tantallus."

Alger immediately entered the name of the vessel into the computer. "That's odd. There's no record of a ship by that name in the log." He frowned. "That name sure sounds familiar, though. It might have been accidentally deleted from the file . . . I don't know."

"This is the Tantallus. We are taking on water! Engine is dead! All onboard navigational systems gone. Drifting. Must receive assistance immediately! Repeat: Must receive assistance immediately."

"Let's go," said Captain Anderson. "Radio coordinates and issue an RAS alert." He checked his watch. "Where is Jeffries?" It would be pitch dark in thirty minutes. Rescue at sea was a dangerous undertaking at best. At night it could be deadly. He barked to Alger for an update on the hurricane.

Bad news, Alger informed him. All radio transmissions were down. "The storm must have taken everything out. Radar too."

Captain Anderson was getting into his raincoat. "There's no telling where that distress call came from. We have no choice but to have a blind look around the ocean."

"Mayday!" The two men fell silent. *"I am going down! Going down! Too much water! Is there anyone out there? Please? Help me!*

Within a few minutes both men were out of the lighthouse and in the truck parked up on the beach. Anderson drove a few miles south to where the coast guard moored a rescue cruiser. He figured the window of opportunity for rescue was about twenty minutes. Alger called the "all clear" and hopped onto the cruiser as Anderson pushed open on the throttle, and the boat charged into the stormy sea.

About a half mile out they picked up another burst from the shortwave radio. "All right!" Anderson shouted. For the first time that afternoon he felt optimistic. The increased clarity of the signal might be an indication they were honing in.

"Keep your eyes open!"

Alger nodded. "Yes, sir."

The boat pitched violently in the gale winds. Rain lashed the deck and roof of the bridge.

"Can anyone hear me?"

The signal was clear now. Anderson felt his heart racing. They had to be close. "There!" shouted Alger, pointing to a small boat bobbing on the horizon.

"That's her!" shouted Anderson

Rocking from side to side, the vessel reminded him of a forlorn buoy. The name *Tantallus* was painted on the hull of the bow. "Ahoy, *Tantallus*!" Anderson yelled as loud as he could. "This is Coast Guard Cutter *Bellingham*!"

The *Tantallus* was tilting drunkenly but otherwise appeared none the worse for wear. He called out again, but there was no answer. Algers scrambled to lash to the crippled vessel as Anderson shut down the engine and unsnapped the emergency medical kit from its mooring. It was not that uncommon for a boat captain to lash himself to a post inside the cabin as a precaution in the case of drowning. It was considered bad luck for a body to be lost at sea. Better for a captain to go down with his boat.

Anderson searched the above deck but failed to find anyone.

"Anything?" he called down to Alger. He could hear the lieutenant rummaging about the cabin below. Alger emerged a few moments later and shook his head. "Must have fallen overboard."

Alger uncoiled the tether and attached a lead wire to the bow of the *Tantallus*. He signaled an OK to the captain, and the engine kicked open and churned homeward.

Suddenly there was a crackling cough on the short-wave radio. Anderson cut the engine immediately.

The voice sounded weary and resigned. *"Repeat. Ship capsized. Death inevitable. No hope of rescue."*

Then came words that made the two men freeze with terror: *"This is the* Tantallus. *Taholah, Washington."*

Anderson looked at Alger in disbelief.

"It c . . . can't be," Alger stammered. "I mean, it d . . . doesn't make any sense . . ."

A bolt of lightening flashed close by, and a loud peal of thunder crackled above. them.

"Cut it loose," the captain ordered.

An eerie silence filled the bridge as the cruiser headed for shore. The lieutenant seemed to be deep in thought. "What's the matter?" Anderson asked.

Alger looked at him. "The *Tantallus*, sir. I remember now. There was a storm that struck a swordfish fleet not too far from here. A couple of boats went down fast, and the crew had to abandon ship. They all drowned. But the captain of the *Tantallus* survived. It was rumored he ran for shore rather than save the crews of the other boats."

"You mean he left them out there to die?"

"Yes, sir."

The captain swallowed hard. "Have you heard the old legend, lieutenant, about the sailor who fails to answer his mates' distress call?"

Alger shook his head.

"Well, according to the legend, he is doomed for eternity to relive the deaths of his mates . . . in a storm-tossed sea."

Lieutenant Alger narrowed his eyes. "You're not suggesting—"

The captain shook his head.

"There's one more thing, sir," Alger said. "The reason I didn't remember the *Tantallus* at first . . ."

"What is it?" demanded the captain.

Alger swallowed hard. "The *Tantallus* sir. It sank in 1947."

Both men looked back, but there was no sign of the *Tantallus.* Not another word was spoken on the rocky ride back to shore.

Ensign Jeffries was having his first coffee when Captain Anderson and Lieutenant Alger entered the lighthouse station. Jeffries gulped when he saw the angry scowl on the captain's face.

"Jeffries!" he barked. "Where the heck have you been?"

"Sir?" sputtered Jeffries. "What do you mean, sir?"

Anderson recognized the look of honest confusion on the young man's face.

Jeffries said, "My shift begins at five, sir."

Lieutenant Alger gently pulled the captain aside. "Look, sir" he said, directing his attention to the clock on the wall.

It read 4:59 P.M.

The captain's eyebrows raised in astonishment.

Lieutenant Alger turned to Jeffries. "What about the hurricane?" he asked.

Jeffries surprised them both. "Hurricane?" He chuckled. "What hurricane?" He gazed out the window. "It's been the most beautiful day of the year."